# Who's at the Zoo?

Story by Michael Pryor
Illustrations by Omar Aranda

## Contents

## Chapter 1

# The Competition

My sister, Maddy, counts everything. She counts the flowers on the wallpaper. She counts the flakes in the cornflakes box. She counts the hairs in Grandpa's nose. Everything! I know she's only five, but this counting *really* gets on my nerves, sometimes. Like the time we went to one of my favourite places – the zoo.

You know how you really look forward to something and then it all goes wrong? It happens to me all the time, and our zoo trip really started going wrong when we got through the crowded zoo entrance. Mum said, "Oliver."

When I heard that, I knew it was trouble. It's always trouble when she calls me "Oliver."

ZOO
ENTRANCE

"Oliver," Mum repeated. "We have a job for you. We know how much you like the zoo, so we want you to look after Maddy and show her all the interesting animals."

Mum explained, "Your father and I want to draw some animals. Make sure you stay close to us, and keep an eye on Maddy."

Mum and Dad are always drawing. Rocks, trees, bits of sky, that sort of stuff. They even used to make *me* hang *their* drawings up on the fridge. Parents! I just can't understand them, sometimes.

"But, but, but – the competition!" I spluttered. "I can't look after Maddy *and* fill out the competition entry form at the same time!"

The competition was the whole reason I'd suggested the zoo trip. It was a chance to win a Lifetime Gold Pass to the zoo, just by answering some questions about zoo animals. When I grow up, I'd like to work with animals, so walking around the zoo is my idea of a good time.

"I'll help you, Ollie," Maddy said. "I'll count all the animals for you."

I groaned.

"Don't look so sad, Ollie," Dad said. "It's going to be a fun day!"

Mum and Dad started to wander off with their sketchbooks and pencils.

I'd seen the results of Mum and Dad's drawings before. Their trees looked like blobs with leaves. Their hills looked like blobs with trees. Their people looked like blobs with hair.

It was good they had a hobby, I supposed.

"Hey," I called to them, after checking my competition form. "The leopards would be good to draw." I took Maddy's hand. "This way!"

Mum and Dad turned to follow us, and we were on our way.

Chapter 2

# Where Are the Armadillos?

"Eighteen, nineteen, twenty," Maddy counted, as we eased past all the people near a kiosk. "Twenty people with ice creams," she announced. "That's a *lot* of ice cream."

"And a lot of mess," I said. I scratched my head. "Which way are the big cats?"

Maddy pointed to a sign. "That way."

When we got to the big cats, Mum and Dad grinned and started talking about the way the lions were stretched out. They flipped open their sketchbooks and soon their pencils were flying across the paper.

“Nine, ten, eleven stripes on that tiger,” Maddy counted. “One, two, three, four adult lions. How many lion cubs are there in the enclosure, Ollie?”

“Five thousand and sixteen,” I mumbled, and got ready to write down my first answer on the competition entry form. “Now, question one: what is the difference between a snow leopard and an ordinary leopard?”

Maddy scratched her nose. “No,” she said.

“No?”

“No. There are five lion cubs. Look! One, two, three …”

I read the sign on the snow leopard enclosure, and then the sign about the other kind of leopard. I scribbled down my answer and read the competition form again.

"Come on, Maddy, I've got to find the armadillos." I waved to Mum and Dad. "I've heard that great artists really like drawing armadillos," I called to them.

"Really?" Mum said. "Where are these armadillos?"

"This way," I pointed, taking a wild guess.

"How far is it?" Maddy asked.

"I don't know!"

"Good. I'll count our steps."

We went past the seals, who were showing off as usual, and then around the bear enclosure. "Goldilocks!" Maddy crowed.

"Pardon?" I asked, while I looked around for the armadillos.

"Look," she pointed. "*Goldilocks and the Three Bears*! That's my favourite fairy tale, because it's got a number in it."

"What about *The Three Little Pigs*?" I asked, as I peered at the sign on the bear enclosure and checked the entry form again. Question six wanted to know what bears ate, so I wrote down the answer.

"Yes." Maddy thought deeply. "That's my favourite. *Goldilocks and the Three Bears* is my second favourite."

Maddy counted the stripes on the zebras, the number of baby antelopes and the number of cameras on the tourists. Mum and Dad did quick blobby sketches of the families wandering around looking at the animals. Almost by accident, I got an answer to question eleven (what kind of gum leaves koalas like best), which was a bit of luck.

I looked at my watch. "Oh, no!" I yelped. "An hour has gone already!"

"How many minutes is that?" Maddy asked.

"Too many. I've still got to find out about the armadillos. Where are they?"

ANTELOPES GIRAFFES
KOALAS ECHIDNAS

Chapter 3

# A World Record Attempt

We had reached a strangely quiet part of the zoo. I couldn't remember exactly how we'd got here. All I could see were empty enclosures, a few sheds and lots of rubbish bins. It looked as empty as school five minutes after the bell at the end of the day.

Mum and Dad strolled over to where an old truck was parked near the wall of the zoo.

"There are no armadillos around here," Maddy said to me.

"She's right," came a voice. "The armadillos are way over the other side of the zoo."

I looked around for the owner of the voice, but I couldn't see anyone. "Hello?" I called. "Can you help us?"

"Sure."

The voice was coming from an enclosure right in the back corner of the zoo. We had to walk past a shed and several rubbish bins before we could see it.

"Perhaps it's a zookeeper cleaning the place out," I said. I waved to Mum and Dad, then Maddy and I trotted over.

As we got closer, we slowed, staring.

"I don't believe it," I whispered.

"What's that TV doing in there, Ollie?" Maddy said. "And those chairs? And that pink rug?" Maddy scratched her nose furiously. She always did that when she was puzzled.

A skinny young man with a ragged red beard jumped up from one of the lounge chairs.

His clothes were loose and baggy.

"Hi, I'm Ric! Thanks for visiting." He smiled brightly. "It's getting pretty lonely stuck way back here."

I stared. A human inside an enclosure instead of an animal? Had the world turned upside down?

"What are you doing in there?" I asked, as Ric used the remote control to turn off his TV. "You're a person!"

"Look at the sign," he said.

I read the sign aloud: "*Homo sapiens.* Human. Found worldwide. DO NOT FEED."

"I'm here to break a world record," Ric explained.

"The zoo wants a human on display for a world record?" I said. "That's silly! The zoo's for animals!"

HOMO SAPIENS
DO NOT FEED

Ric shrugged. "It was my idea. The London Zoo had someone on display for a week. The Central City Museum had someone in an exhibit for two weeks. I'm going to beat that record by being on display for a whole month. The zoo will get some good publicity, and I'll be famous!"

"So you'll be famous for doing something silly," I said.

"Maybe it's not so silly," Ric said. "Humans are part of the animal kingdom, after all, and sometimes people need reminding of that. So here I am, in my natural surroundings."

Maddy spoke up. "That's why you have one TV, one lamp, three lounge chairs, one …"

In a small voice, Maddy went on counting, pointing at each piece of furniture in the enclosure. It was very well set up.

HOMO SA
O NOT F

"So, you're aiming to break a world record," I said to Ric. "How's it going?"

Ric sighed. His shoulders slumped. "It's tough. I didn't realise how boring it would be. People come and look at me, snap a few pictures and point, and that's it. No one talks to me. It's as if I'm some sort of animal!"

"Isn't that the point?"

Ric didn't hear me. He threw his hands up in the air. "And the food! It's awful! No pies, no hamburgers, no hot dogs with mustard! The zookeepers say they're making sure I stay in tip-top shape." He looked as if he was going to cry.

I shook my head. "It sounds awful, Ric. I wish I could help."

He looked hopeful. "Have you got some chips? A doughnut?"

"Sorry."

Ric slumped against the enclosure glass. "Oh well. I suppose I'll just go and watch TV." He waved gloomily and trudged back to his chair.

I felt sad for Ric, but we needed to keep going. "Come on, Maddy." I tugged at her hand. "I still have to find the armadillo enclosure."

Maddy pointed at a sign. "Does that say 'armadillos'?"

I hurried over to Mum and Dad. "They say that the true test of an artist is whether they can draw an armadillo properly," I said.

Mum and Dad shared a look. "Which way?" Dad asked, and I led the way.

When we got to the armadillo enclosure, I wrote down that armadillos come from North and South America.

"Come on! The monkeys!" I said, stuffing my pencil in my pocket.

"I've hardly started my armadillo drawing!" Mum protested.

"A quick sketch is a good sketch!" I said. "This way!"

ARMADILLOS

We sprinted to the monkeys and apes, which were near the zoo gates. My last question on the entry form was, "What is the second-largest great ape?" I scribbled "Orangutan" and that was that.

Complete! I could see that Lifetime Gold Pass already!

Chapter 4

# An Escape!

"Warning! Warning!" the loudspeaker above our head suddenly boomed. "All members of the public, please leave the zoo! We've had an escape! Do not panic!"

In seconds, people were running towards the zoo exit, screaming and shouting.

"Wild tiger!" someone yelled.

"Escaped crocodile!" another shrieked.

"Angry tortoise!" someone else wailed.

I panicked a little bit, but I think I hid it from Maddy while Mum and Dad tried to sketch the fleeing crowd. What sort of animal had escaped? A lion? A bear? This was serious!

Maddy put her hands on her hips. "Why is everyone running from Ric?" she asked.

"Who's Ric?" Mum asked.

I explained who Ric was and about his record-breaking attempt. Maddy added, "He didn't like the food, though. That's why he left his enclosure, I suppose."

I looked in the direction Maddy was looking.

Three zookeepers were helping Ric the human back to his enclosure. Ric had a doughnut in one hand, a milkshake in the other and a hamburger in his mouth. Another zookeeper followed them, and he had a megaphone. "It's all right, folks!" he said. "No wild animals are loose! Just a hungry human!"

"He's going to have to start his record-breaking attempt all over again," I said, sadly.

"You know what?" Maddy chirped, as we watched Ric gobbling down his treats. "I'm sick of counting things. I'm going to read everything instead. Those signs first. Zoo, Entrance, Exit. Here, Ollie, let me read that." I handed her my entry form.

"Ollie, what day is it?"

"It's Sunday," I said.

"Not the day. What's the date?"

"It's the sixteenth," I told her. "Why?"

"The closing date for entries is the fourteenth," Maddy pointed out. "That's what it says here."

"Oh, no!" I sat on the footpath and put my head in my hands. "No Lifetime Gold Pass!"

"Don't move," Mum said. "Stay right where you are."

"What?" I froze. "Is there a dangerous animal sneaking up on me?"

"No," Dad said. "You're in the perfect pose for a sketch. It shouldn't take more than an hour or two."

"Don't worry, Ollie." Maddy patted me on the shoulder. "I'll read all the little printed rules and conditions to you from your competition entry form."

I groaned again.